Pout Party

by

Sarah McColl

Brooklyn NY

One sunny, shining, beautiful day,
Rue woKe up feeling grouchy and gray.

The light was too bright,
her breakfast too crunchy.
Her shoes were too tight,
and her socks were too bunchy.

Mom said, "Cheer up!"
and gave her a kiss,
but she stomped off to school
with a growl and a hiss.

In class she was snippy,
snappish, and sour.

When Teacher said,
"Smile!"
Rue gave her a glower.

The songs were all glum;
the lessons a bore.
Nap time was dreary.
The games were a chore.

With her friends she was prickly,
bad-tempered, and rude.

"Let's play a game!" they said

"I'm just not in the mood."

By the time recess came,
she just wanted to shout:

"No one understands!
I JUST WANT TO POUT!"

"I don't want to be cheered,
and I don't want to play."

So she picked up her pencil
and made a display:

I'm having a
Pout Party.
You are all invited.
No games, no cake.
Don't be happy or
excited.

She stomped to the playground
and put up her note.

Her friends gathered close
to see what she wrote.

"That doesn't sound fun."

"I would rather go play!"

So they did—except Joy—
who decided to stay.

She thought that Rue
seemed a little bit lonely.

"Welcome to my Pout Party,
grumpy faces only!"

Her nose went SCRUNCH!
Her eyebrows went ZIP!
Then she heaved a big grunt
and stuck out her lip.

Rue had to admit,
"That's a pretty good pout.
But I'm the best frowner,
so you'd better watch out!"

She took a deep breath
and with all of her power,
she summoned the grumpiest,
gloomiest glower.

"That's great!" said Joy,

"but I've got you beat."

She grumbled
and groaned
and stomped
with her feet.

"That looks sort of fun!"

"Can I try, too?"

Before long the whole class was pouting with Rue.

"You've got to be grouchier!
Puff out your pout!"

"Make your shoulders slouchier!"

"Stick your forehead out!"

Their stomping and grumbling
all looked sort of silly.

The faces they made—
well, they looked funny, really!

They made such a ruckus
as Rue looked around,
she stifled the tiniest
giggling sound.

But her giggle then grew,
and started to spread.

They laughed and they howled
till their faces were red.

Rue felt better
than ever before.

"I don't think that I need to pout anymore."

When recess was done,
she lined up with her friends.

"The Pout Party was fun!
We should do that again."

And Joy said:

"Rue, if you ever feel cruddy
you don't need to worry,
I'll still be your buddy!"

"Well, if anyone else feels like having a pout, I think that it's just fine to let it all out."

For my partner Kaighin and for Beulah,
who has a most excellent pout.

POUT PARTY

Text and Illustrations © Sarah McColl 2022

Published by POW!
a division of powerHouse Packaging & Supply, Inc.
32 Adams Street, Brooklyn, NY 11201-1021

www.POWKidsbooks.com
Distributed by powerHouse Books
www.powerHouseBooks.com

First edition, 2022

Library of Congress Control Number: 2022941539

ISBN 978-1-64823-017-2

Printed by Toppan Leefung

10 9 8 7 6 5 4 3 2 1

Printed and bound in China